Aurora

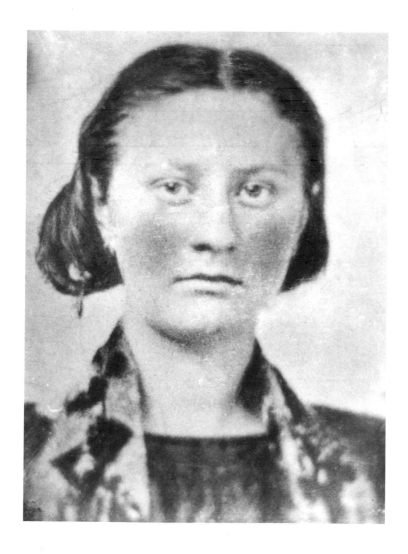

Aurora
Daughter of the Dawn

◆　　◆　　◆

A Story of New Beginnings

J. J. Kopp

With drawings by Clark Moor Will
Afterword by Jane Kirkpatrick

Oregon State University Press
Corvallis

Aurora Colony Historical Society
Aurora

The paper in this book meets the guidelines for permanence
and durability of the Committee on Production Guidelines
for Book Longevity of the Council on Library Resources
and the minimum requirements of the American National
Standard for Permanence of Paper for Printed Library
Materials Z39.48-1984.

Library of Congress Cataloging-in-Publication Data
Kopp, James J.
  Aurora, daughter of the dawn : a story of new beginnings /
J.J. Kopp ; with drawings by Clark Moor Will.
    p. cm.
  ISBN 978-0-87071-671-3 (alk. paper) ~ ISBN 978-0-87071-672-
0 (e-book)
  1. Aurora Colony (Marion County, Or.)~Juvenile fiction. I.
Will, Clark M. (Clark Moore), 1893-1982. II. Title.
  PZ7.K83617Au 2012
  [Fic]~dc23
                                    2012015118

First published in 2012 by Oregon State University Press and
    Aurora Colony Historical Society
Printed in the United States of America

Oregon State University Press
121 The Valley Library
Corvallis OR 97331-4501
541-737-3166 • fax 541-737-3170
www.osupress.oregonstate.edu

All beings live in one light only
So does every eye of nature
And the whole history of the world
Preaches about nothing but Aurora

Aurora, Aurora you lovely light
When you come return
Forget me not

First verse and chorus of song titled Aurora, written by Wilhelm Keil, verses of which appear at the beginning of each chapter

Contents

Aurora

Dawn

As soon as the golden dawn
Comes up above mountain and valley
Then every life preaches
The love of God all over

Papa says my arrival in this mortal world was a new beginning. Papa says that every day is a new beginning and every day is heralded by the dawn. Thus he chose to name me Aurora as the daughter of the dawn, for Aurora is the goddess of the dawn. But Papa is a Christian man and leads his own flock of believers so he did not want my name to be seen as some pagan symbol. Rather he wants my name and my presence here as a mortal to be a symbol of new beginnings. I like that and my life has been very full of new beginnings.

◆　◆　◆

It is December 1862 in the Aurora colony and I am very sick from something that Mama calls the pox. Several of my brothers and sisters are sick too, some worse than me. Mama and other women from the community tend to us. They try to keep our heads cool with damp cloths but the cloths hurt the sores on my face. They also try to keep us warm but I am too hot to lie under the many quilts that they have piled on me, and I am always kicking these off, much to Mama's dislike. She does not say a harsh word but asks me to be still and the fever and sores will go away. Mama looks tired and sad herself as she moves between me and my older sisters, Louisa—named after Mama—and Gloriunda, as they lie beside me and also kick off their covers. Mama says Elias and others also had the pox but she does not speak of how they are doing.

As I lie as still as a thirteen-year-old girl can, Mama tells me to think about times past and see what I can remember of the new beginnings in my life. At first I thought this was child's play but as I moved between sleep and kicking covers I started to remember what I could of my life as Aurora Keil.

◆　◆　◆

Of course, I do not remember the day I was born—March 18, 1849—and very little of my early years. But I can remember through stories told me by Papa, Mama, and my older brothers and sisters, as well as others who were there at the time of my birth and for many years before and after. In fact, I probably remember these stories as much as I remember things myself.

I was born in Bethel, Missouri, where Papa had brought together a group of Christian believers to live in what was called a colony, doing things together and following the Golden Rule. I did not know what the Golden Rule was or meant until I was seven or so but I do remember Papa talking about it frequently when he spoke to the colony people on Sundays and to us children at home. Mama explained it to me as caring for each other person as if they were Jesus. I remember asking her once when I was very little if this meant my brothers too and she laughed loudly—something she used to do before we lost Willie—and said especially your brothers.

Mama said that Papa began the Bethel Colony about the time Louisa was born, in 1844. Mama and Papa had come to America from the Old Country, that I later learned meant Bavaria, in the mid-1830s and lived in the large city of New York for some time before moving to Pittsburgh, where Willie was born in January 1837. Papa was a tailor but also familiar with healing and offered both his services to those who needed mending of clothes or mending of their bodies. While in Pittsburgh he also became interested in the mending of souls, as Mama says, and tried to preach in some of the regular churches there but Papa did not like to be controlled by the rules of others so he decided to start his own congregation and found those who would follow.

As Mama told me, she was busy starting her own congregation by bringing children into the world. After Willie, there was

August, and then Frederick, who Papa calls Fritz. Elias—or Eli as Papa calls him— was born as Papa was planning to send a group of scouts from Pittsburgh to the frontier to find a place for his group of followers so they could live separate from the temptations of life in the cities of the East. They found such a place in Missouri and Papa, Mama, and the four children moved there, where Louisa soon joined the family. Many families and others interested in what Papa preached also moved to Missouri. Papa named the place Bethel, that he says means the House of God. Mama says that Bethel became a good place to raise a family and to live with others in a Christian way. The settlement grew and so did our family, as Gloriunda arrived and then I became the seventh child. Two more Keil children were born at Bethel—my younger sister Amelia and then baby Emmanuel. Although I was too small to remember much, I do have memories of little Emmanuel joining our family. I think Papa was glad to have another boy after four girls. Emmanuel made us a family of nine children, a number that Mama said was just right. But Mama says just about anything is just right. That is the way she is.

◆　◆　◆

Thinking about my family makes me feel warm inside—different than the warmth of the quilts that I want to kick off or my fever that I want to go away. I don't want to kick off these memories or have them go away. Mama was right that remembering is a good way to spend my time here in bed as I get better. I will do more of this after I rest some. The gentle rain on the roof sings me a lullaby as I close my eyes.

◆　◆　◆

1853

All beings lay in deep slumber
As in the gray night of death
Everyone felt his grief
Before Aurora did awake

Some of my earliest memories of life in the Bethel community were of that large house called Elim, which was home to our family but also a gathering place for many others in the colony. Papa and the men would sit in one of the rooms for discussions and to smoke their pipes. I mostly remember the smells of the room where the men met as Gloriunda and I would sometimes sneak into the room after the men left. I am sure that Papa would not approve and we know that Mama did not as she caught us coming from the room late one afternoon. She scolded us harshly but it seemed like she had given this sermon before. Gloriunda and I had strong suspicions that one of the boys—perhaps Willie—had told Mama of our escapade.

I also remember the hustling and bustling of the women doing the work in the kitchen of the house, making bread, preparing meals, and making candles. Those smells come to mind and they are much nicer than the smell of stale smoke in the room where the men met.

◆　◆　◆

As I lie here in this darkened room with one small candle flickering in the corner, I am eager to get up and go down to the kitchen in our new big house in Aurora. At times I can smell the bread cooking or hear the voices of the women helping to prepare meals. I ask Mama when I can get up to go help and she always says soon.

◆　◆　◆

Mama is an excellent cook and she was helped at Bethel (and here too) in the kitchen by my older sisters as well as several of the unmarried women of the colony. When I was too young to help with the cooking, there were still things for me to do to help out. One was to watch after Amelia—just a year younger

16

than me though she didn't take to my ordering her around—
and Emmanuel who was just an infant. Later I learned that even
though Mama had told me to watch over my younger siblings,
each of my older sisters had been given the same assignment for
those younger than her. And I suspect Mama even told Amelia
that her job was to watch over Emmanuel. But it was probably
best that we watched over each other in such a large family.

The young unmarried women who helped at Elim also
assisted in keeping watch over the Keil children, although
Willie, August, Fritz, and Eli often were out working with the
men in the fields or in one of the other regular labors of the
colony. We each had a favorite among the women who tended
to us. Mine was the young Wagner girl, Emma, who often was
at the house even when she did not have responsibilities for
caring for us. She would say that she liked being at Elim because
there was always something happening there, and indeed there
was. Emma was thirteen years older than me but for some
reason we became close, perhaps because, as Mama would later
say, we were of the same cloth. Although Mama had four girls

of her own, I think she was very fond of Emma as well; perhaps she too was of the same cloth.

◆　◆　◆

I remember the day that Emma told us she was going to go with Christian Giesy, her new husband, and a few other men to a faraway place to look for a new home for the colony. Papa may have told us about the scout party but it had no meaning for me until I learned that Emma was to be part of it. This made me very sad and even Mama telling me that this was a new beginning for Emma and possibly for all of us did not make me feel better. It was only after Emma took me aside and told me that I needed to be strong as she expected me to grow up to be just like her that I started to feel some better. Before Emma left she gave me a small needlepoint as a gift but she said it was not finished, so she wanted me to keep it and give it to her when I saw her again so she could finish it.

◆　◆　◆

The completed needlepoint of forget-me-nots sits on the table near my bed now where I am resting. Mama told me the story once that this flower got its name because it cried out to Adam and Eve as they left the Garden of Eden—"Forget me not." The needlepoint reminds me of the flowers at Elim but also all the flowers I have seen since and those along the streams here at Aurora. When I am well, I am going to make a quilt of flowers, perhaps of the sunflowers; I like them most as they stand so proud but also because they turn toward the sun at dawn.

◆　◆　◆

I knew Mama was going to miss Emma too. Emmanuel was just a baby then, having arrived shortly before Yuletide the previous year. Amelia was not quite three years old, and Mama appreciated the help Emma provided. Many of the other women helped Mama and she was grateful for that but, as Mama would tell me later when we moved to Oregon, some people just like some cloth pieces tend to go together better than others in making a quilt. But Mama also said that it takes many different cloth pieces to complete a quilt. Each part helps to keep the larger piece together, held by a common thread. I think Mama meant that Papa was the common thread but I think of Mama as the common thread for our family and for the women of the colony.

◆　◆　◆

I remember the day the scout party left to head west, mostly because of a tearful goodbye to Emma as I clung to Mama's skirt as she too stood with a tear in her eye. Mama tried to console me by telling me it was a new beginning for Emma but I only saw it as an end of something special. My sadness was softened some by the powerful words that Papa spoke to the party and to all the community. I do not recall what he said but I remember the sound of his voice capturing the attention of all present, even the horses and other animals. Papa had a way of making his voice seem like a trumpet as it called out to his people. Then Papa also blew his trumpet to send the scout party on its way as we waved our final goodbyes. My gloom briefly turned to mirth as I saw Willie hurry alongside the scout party as it left Bethel. He was riding one of the old mules—the one with the shorter right front leg so it limped along as best it could while Willie sat proudly atop it pretending to blow his own trumpet. Willie was excited about the promise of this new beginning and his zeal for a moment made Emma's departure a little more bearable.

◆　◆　◆

1854

But soon the deity did turn up
She who is resplendent in gold and silver
She who was in the east her residence
And in the west sank down

Although I was just five years old I remember the day Willie came running into the big house at Elim shouting, "They're back! They're back!" I did not know who they were even after Mama got Willie to calm down enough to explain his outburst, but over time I came to understand the importance of his news, particularly to Willie. They were Joseph and Adam Knight, who were two of the scouts sent west the previous year with Christian Giesy and, of course, Emma. They had just ridden into Bethel after a journey back from Washington Territory where the other members of the scout party had remained. Papa had told us that letters from Christian Giesy had come and told of the land selected for a possible new location for the colony. And Christian had reported that the Knights would be returning to Bethel.

All of this was way beyond my comprehension or interest at the time but I was struck with Willie's giddiness at the news and, to a lesser degree, the reactions of August, Elias, and Frederick, which seemed to be more in response to Willie's actions than their own unbridled enthusiasm. What was of interest to my five-year-old mind was the news that Mama shared with me and the other girls: that Emma Giesy had a baby soon after they arrived in Washington Territory. Mama said she didn't even know Emma was with child when the journey began and perhaps this is why Christian had not told of this news in his reports to Papa.

I'm not sure how I felt at that time about this news. I was glad to hear of Emma but the thought of her with her own child made me feel like something was taken away from me. Emma had been like a member of the family, at least to me, and now she had a family of her own. It was a new beginning for her but the news made me feel as I had when Emma rode off with the scout party. I did not tell Mama this, as I think she would have scolded me for feeling this way, so I kept quiet and tried not to think of Emma or the new land far, far away.

◆ ◆ ◆

I lie here now thinking how childishly I acted at that time and so contrary to the Golden Rule that was central to our community and our family. But since I didn't even know what the Golden Rule meant at that age, I probably should not be so hard on myself. Still, I am ashamed for feeling that way toward a dear friend.

◆ ◆ ◆

The colonists at Bethel were all abuzz about what the arrival of the Knight brothers might mean for each of them. We had just celebrated ten years since the founding of Bethel by Papa, with the band playing and a festival of food and merriment. Now there was the uncertainty of whether we would remain at Bethel or join the scout party in a place called Willapa.

This was not something steadily on my mind but it was spoken of often by various groups. The women who helped Mama talked of this in hushed voices while my brothers— except Emmanuel—spoke of it loudly and often. My older sisters, like the women in the kitchen or out on the porch tending to chores, were less vocal about it but they did get caught up in the boys' play of a wagon train to the west. Willie would hook up the lame mule to one of the small wagons and tell the other children to climb in for the ride to Willapa. He would lift Amelia and Emmanuel up to Louisa or Gloriunda for the make-believe journey. Willie would drive the wagon while Frederick or Eli marched alongside watching for Indians or wolves. If Papa would catch Willie doing this he would tell him this was frivolous but he did not forbid him to do it, as

I think he saw the excitement in his son's eyes. Mama would look on from the porch and wave as this one-wagon train went down and back up the road in front of the big house but with a worried smile on her face.

◆　◆　◆

I miss some of these youthful games or make-believe times we all would have. There were, of course, many other children at Bethel and here at Aurora too, but when we did something as a family—all nine of us children—it was very special and memorable. Since arriving in Aurora such times do not happen often even if they could, as we are missing someone and the older boys or girls are often too busy with helping out for such playful times. Growing older offers many new beginnings but we set aside other things that make us happy in a special way.

◆　◆　◆

1855

Sweet dreams I had
Which no eye did ever see
Therefore you could not hesitate
Till He did revive her

Willie was so excited about the westward journey. I was still too young to understand what this new beginning was all about but I was excited because Willie was. Willie turned eighteen that January, about the time Papa announced that the Lord had instructed him that nearly half of the colonists at Bethel would be packing their belongings and moving to the new Eden that Christian Giesy and others had found in Washington Territory.

We would leave in the late spring when the snow on the high mountains was gone. I knew what snow was as we had it frequently in Bethel, sometimes in harsh blizzards, but never in the late spring or summer. I didn't understand about the high mountains. Later when we started our journey I remember the awe I had for those majestic peaks looming ahead of us on the trail and I wondered why God put them there and not in Missouri.

◆ ◆ ◆

There was increasing excitement about the move west for many of us although much sadness too about leaving friends and some of our family in our home at Bethel. I remember being puzzled by this excitement and sadness but I could feel it in many others, especially Mama. She worked hard to prepare our family for the move but her sadness at the idea of leaving Elim, our home at Bethel, was always there too. But she knew Papa would not make us move if it was not what the Lord wanted and she reminded us children many times that this was a new beginning. And Mama said there were many places in the scriptures where people left their home to seek a new home in a distant land.

Soon after my sixth birthday Papa announced when we would leave for our new Eden and that there would be twenty-five or so wagons as part of our train. Preparations were heightened and along with them Willie's excitement about the adventure ahead. He told Papa over and over that he wanted to ride in the lead wagon and, if Papa would allow, to blow the trumpet to signal the start of each day's travel. Papa assured Willie that he could ride in the lead wagon but he was not so sure about the trumpet. Papa said that was something only he should do as others might think he no longer was the leader. But Willie told me that he thought Papa would allow it, maybe not all the time but now and then. This thought made Willie beam even more, and I was so happy for Willie.

♦ ♦ ♦

A soft moan from across the room brings me back to the present and the dim light from the hallway does not let me see if it is Gloriunda or Louisa who has made the noise. It is soon quiet again and I return to my reflections in the mirror of the past.

♦ ♦ ♦

As May arrived, and with it the warmer, sticky days—and the pesky mosquitoes—everyone was anxious about the departure date. But Willie's enthusiasm, although still strong, seemed to be drawn away, as was his level of energy. He grew tired easily and a week before we were to begin our trip he nearly fainted while helping to feed the oxen. Mama put him to bed where he lay for several days, calling out as he dreamed in a voice that still makes me shiver as I lie in my bed. When he was awake and could talk, his only remarks were to remind Papa that he was to be in the lead wagon. Mama told us later that Papa had the men prepare a special bed in the lead wagon for Willie if he did not get well before we left. So Papa was keeping his promise.

And then Willie cried out no more and the quiet from his bed passed through all the community, and only the sounds of the animals were all that we could hear. I remember Mama coming to us children with tears in her eyes and telling us that Willie had started another journey. We did not see Papa for a day or two as he worked quietly at his desk. Mama said he was writing a song for Willie. Outside, others slowly and somberly continued with the preparations for the trip west.

◆　◆　◆

It was on a Wednesday—May 23, 1855—that we finally left Bethel. We were delayed a few days while the lead wagon was changed, not to carry a bed for Willie but to hold a box in which Willie would rest. Mama says the woodworkers made the box special for Willie and that they lined it with metal to keep Willie safe. I did not understand that at the time but I did not question Mama as she seemed so sad.

Papa had finished his song for Willie and, as the wagon train started down the road through the colony with Willie's wagon in the lead pulled by the two mules, Queen and Kate, many started to sing this song. It was a sad song but hearing the voices of many—those who were leaving as well as those who were staying—made the song seem less sad in some way. It perhaps was because they were all singing for Willie.

◆　◆　◆

I lie quiet for a while listening to that song once more in my head. The song is beautiful but I would much rather have Willie than a song. But still, a song is something that can last for a long time and with it the memories of when it was first sung or, as with this song, the person being remembered. A song is like a new beginning each time it is sung—a new beginning of memories, a new beginning of hope.

◆　◆　◆

"Willie
goes before
and we follow"
Dec.9.1897

"at the sound of
my trumpet"

What I remember most of the journey from Bethel to our new
beginnings in Washington Territory is, of course, the wagon
with Willie leading the way and thinking of Willie in the
wooden box. I knew Mama always said that Willie was with our
savior in a much better place, but why then was this box on the
wagon in front of our little train. How could Willie be there
and with our savior?

❖   ❖   ❖

My first thrilling experience on the journey was when we
had to cross the Missouri River. It was a great stream that I
could not see across. And I remember how brown the water
looked, almost the color of some of the horses and cattle. The
wagons were loaded on a ferry that was barely above the water
and rocked with the movement of the river. The animals were
driven upstream to a place where they had to swim across the
water. I was glad I did not have to see the oxen, cattle, mules,
and horses trying to swim across that huge river, as I would
have been frightened they might wash away and drown.

I stayed in the wagon and tried not to look out at the water but Fritz and Elias teased me for being so frightened. But I noticed that they kept far away from the edges of the floating island so I knew they were not as brave as their words. It took six hours to cross the river and, when we reached the other side, it was the most joy I had felt in some time. Later Mama said that crossing the river was an important sign of a new beginning as it was like reaching a new land. Even though she was still saddened by Willie's death, I thought that this river crossing brought a little more life back to her.

◆　◆　◆

I also remember Papa blowing his horn when we started each day's travels or at other times to gather people. And I thought of Willie's hope that he too might be able to announce the beginning of the next stage of the journey with a trumpet blast. Papa also would sound the trumpet to impress the many Indians we saw on our journey. Papa would say that we were

...the wagons were hand pushed onto Steam Ferry—

safe among the Indians as we were all in the hands of God. Others spoke fearfully of trouble with the Indians, as they did not like the many wagons passing through their country. But we had no trouble and Papa often invited Indians to come to our camp and to sup with us. Once a tall Indian man with his many sons came to eat with Papa and he gave them food to take to the mother and other children. I saw Papa make this Christian gesture so I gave the man the blanket I was carrying. The Indian man smiled and Papa looked at me with a little

...."trumpets were sounded"—

"We saw an Indian"

smile that showed he was pleased by my generosity but the frown in his eyes told me that I should not be so foolhardy with things we might need ourselves.

◆ ◆ ◆

There are many other things I remember of that time although it seems so long ago. The journey itself seemed to take forever and I had forgotten what our home had been like in Missouri before we had been on the trail very long. We came upon the man I called baby buggy man as he was traveling by himself with all his belongings in a baby buggy. I always wondered what had happened to the baby or to its mother but no one told me that story. The baby buggy man spoke German and Papa allowed him to travel with us if he would help with the animals, which he was happy to do as he seemed so alone. One must get tired of pushing a baby buggy along the rough trail, and a baby buggy does not talk or sing or laugh with you.

❖   ❖   ❖

I remember the animals we had with us and the many new and different animals we saw. The dogs we took from Bethel seemed like part of the family and at times I could tolerate them more than my brothers. The dogs were our guardians at night—our angels of safety, as Papa said, as they would alert us to visitors, whether they were Indians, other travelers, or unwanted creatures seeking our food or more. I grew very fond of one dog that we called Pony, because he pranced like a proud horse. I was very sad when Pony did not come with us after we stopped at one of the trading posts. I do not know if he ran away or someone took him but I missed Pony. I did not need any other sorrow to remind me of the box on the lead wagon. Other dogs would join us as we went and eventually I came to like a stray dog that we called Rink but not in the same way as Pony.

❖   ❖   ❖

Seeing the buffalo in large herds was a shock and a joy. There were so many together at times that it seemed like the prairie itself was moving as the herd roamed. The men and the dogs would go to hunt the buffalo and I was worried about the dogs running beneath the legs of those huge animals. I didn't seem to be as concerned for the men on the horses and mules, perhaps because they had guns. I was sorry that these animals had to be killed but Papa and Mama both said it was important that we had that meat. And Papa would say, as he often did about things, that God put the buffalo here for our needs. I

..... a rare sight,
Pronghorns at close range....

don't think God intended for my older brothers to scare me with buffalo skulls and bones that they found frequently along the trail.

We saw other wild animals, including deer and the majestic elk, when we reached the mountains. I was excited to see the graceful pronghorn antelope and some were brave enough to come close to the wagon train. There were all sorts of birds along the trail, more than I could count. The boys would always

be telling stories of animals they had seen or heard, or whose tracks they had followed. These ranged from smaller critters such as raccoons, badgers, and possums to larger beasts such as coyotes, cougars, bears, and wolves. I had seen some signs of this from the trail and a few coyotes came close enough to camp that I could see them as they looked for food. I heard the wolves at night, especially in the mountains, where their howls would echo through the canyons. But I had not encountered a wild beast up close and had no real desire for that experience. My brothers, however, said it was only a matter of time before this happened and said it may happen when you least expect it.

◆   ◆   ◆

It was one warm night in the mountains when you could see the lightning in the distance and hear the thunder as it rolled through the valleys. I was used to strong storms like this as we had them frequently at Bethel but the way each thunder clap continued to bounce from one side of the mountains to the other was something new and alarming to me. It was like the mountains were singing a sad song in a deep voice. I lay awake on my bedroll under the wagon listening to this song that was hardly a lullaby. Then I heard another noise coming from the edge of our camp and the noise seemed to be getting closer.

The moon that had been bright earlier when we crawled into our sleeping space—bed is a word I wouldn't use for some time—was now hidden behind storm clouds. The campfires that were still burning cast some light but produced more flickering shadows that did not ease my anxiety. I tried to listen to see if Mama or my sisters beside me were awake but I only heard quiet, steady breathing. And still the noise came closer. Then it stopped. I lay perfectly still but then I started to feel the presence of something near to my leg. I did not want to scream

or jump in fear that this would surely cause the wild animal to attack, as my brothers said it would. I could then hear some soft panting that got louder as it moved closer to my face. I lay paralyzed with fear and thought of all the stories that the boys had told.

Then in one instant there was a wet lick on my face that finally caused me to scream, which in turn caused those nearest me to scream also, and Mama jumped up so quickly she hit her head on the bottom of the wagon. Others asleep in the wagon, including three of my brothers, who took turns with us girls in sleeping in the wagon, also jumped to life to see what the commotion was. Papa appeared with a stern and worried look to see what was causing this ruckus. As Mama bent over me, holding one hand on her bruised brow, I told her that a wild animal licked my face. She told Papa and Papa told others but no one, even the two men who were supposed to be on watch, had seen an animal of any kind or any sign of one. Even the dogs had not made a fuss as they always did when an intruder approached camp. Mama said I must have been having a bad dream but I told her I was not asleep. The boys giggled loudly nearby and talked of Aurora's encounter with a fierce mountain lion until Papa told them to hush.

It took some time for things to calm down and I moved closer to Mama, who was still rubbing where she had bumped her head. Neither she nor I slept much the rest of the night; we held hands and listened to the thunder take its music further away. With my other hand I rubbed my cheek where something had given me what I assumed was a friendly lick. As the early light of the dawn finally ended the long night, Mama leaned over me as she got up to prepare the morning meal and whispered, "Maybe it was Willie's angel giving you a kiss."

The incident didn't stop my brothers telling their stories of wild animals but I knew that I had the best story. Then Elias got chased by one of the oxen and the other stories weren't told as often.

◆   ◆   ◆

Still today I don't know what it was that licked me, but I do know that I was not dreaming. I raise my hand from under the heavy covers to touch my face, moist now not from a mysterious lick but from the sweat from the fever, and wonder what it

"We were now thru the mountains"

could have been. I wanted to think it was Pony that came back to us, which is perhaps why the other dogs did not bark, but there was no sign of him after that night. Maybe my screams scared him away again.

◆　◆　◆

The oxen and the mules were some of the most important animals on our trip as they did the hard work of pulling the wagons and carrying loads. They had to struggle to ford many streams that we crossed and to deal with hot days as well as muddy trails when the weather turned bad. Several oxen died as we went through the mountains and it was very sad to see them lying beside the trail as we moved on. We had to adjust and help each other.

◆　◆　◆

Later, after we crossed many rivers and many mountains, we came to a place where the Indians had many horses and some of

Aurora + Cosmo
..... top of page 206, Skiff 1935
"The Chief gave my little girl a string of pearls." Clark Moor Will 4/21/1951

the most beautiful ponies I had ever seen. Papa wished to trade for the horses but many of the Indians did not wish to trade. Later Papa met with several chiefs who not only were willing to trade but wished to give each of my brothers a horse. Because of this Fritz, August, and Elias each got a pony. Emmanuel was too small. This made me think of how excited Willie would be if he received a horse from an Indian chief. But I was more excited as one chief walked over from his own horse and took something from a small leather bag. He reached out and presented me with a beautiful string of beads. I was overcome with joy at this gesture and I still am when I think of it and see the beads hanging from a small hook over my bed now.

◆　◆　◆

When we came to the river that was called the Columbia I was both thrilled and frightened by this mighty stream. It was thrilling as I remembered the stories that were told of the Lewis and Clark expedition fifty years earlier and the joy they had felt in getting to this river that they knew flowed into the Pacific Ocean. That made me and many of the others in our wagon train share similar feelings of joy but it also made me uneasy to think about the end of this journey and what it might bring.

Although I knew that this truly was a new beginning, as Mama repeatedly reminded us, I wondered the beginning of what. And I also knew that the end of the journey would mean that Willie's travels on this earth would come to an end also. I didn't know what Papa was going to do with the box with Willie inside it but I knew that it could not stay on the wagon that carried it from Bethel. So seeing the Columbia River and traveling beside it for many days brought different feelings of joy and sadness.

The size of the river itself and its powerful waters also made me wary. I understood that we would have to cross it at some point and seeing the many cascades and the large waterfalls did not help my uneasiness. It was fascinating to see the Indians fishing right among the falls at one section of the river where it starts into a great canyon but the idea of floating on such a river was alarming.

◆　◆　◆

When we arrived at the place called The Dalles, it was a time of joy and, for me, of fear. It was joyous as one of the first to meet us was Christian Giesy, who had come from the new site for the colony to direct us there. There was much excitement as we greeted the lead scout and Christian looked greatly relieved that our party had arrived safely. I wanted to ask him about Emma but there were more important matters at hand.

One was that it was apparent that the time had come to face my fears of crossing the great river, as the canyon became too narrow to continue on land. We needed to load the wagon on a flatboat and go ourselves on a steamboat. Papa sent some men with the animals by a land trail but it was too rugged for the wagons. Then my fear grew. Just as we were preparing to depart, Papa was taken away by some men and we all, even Mama, were in tears as we did not know what was happening. We shoved off without Papa and our uncertainty of where the river was taking us was only made more evident in Papa's absence.

Matters turned worse on the second day on the river when an immense storm came up the great canyon and waves washed over the sides of our boat. We looked on in frightened amazement as it appeared that the flatboat with our wagons might wash away. Willie's wagon was on the flatboat and I wondered if we would lose Willie once again. But almost as quickly as the storm came upon us, it was over and the skies cleared. Shortly after that we went ashore to check for damage and to calm our nerves.

While we rested another steamboat appeared and seeing us along the shore came to where we were. We were overjoyed to see Papa on the deck with Mr. Charles Ruge, the colony teacher and we rushed to the edge of the water to greet them. Mama was overcome and wept silently. We all felt the crossing of a river had once more been a sign, and Papa's return to us only made that sign seem more powerful. We were at a new beginning and all would be well now.

◆ ◆ ◆

It was not until much later that Mama explained to us younger children why Papa had not left The Dalles with us. The soldiers had taken him away because he was accused of providing aid to the Indians—some of whom were at war with American troops in Washington Territory—and of making statements to the Indians that Americans could not be trusted. It is true that Papa provided food and some supplies to the Indians but this was a gesture he made to others in need that we encountered on the trail. If Papa was arrested for this, I should have been arrested for giving away my blanket! And Papa would not say anything bad about the United States, for he was proud to be an American now and all of his children had been born in this country. The officer in charge quickly realized that the comments made about Papa were false. It turned out that they were made by two men that Papa had taken in at Fort Laramie of his own Christian kindness and brought to the Oregon Territory. They went to work for the Indian agent at The Dalles and brought these accusations against Papa. A quick trial in which Mr. Ruge testified on behalf of Papa ended with Papa being sent free and the accusers receiving public scorn. Papa and Mr. Ruge then hastened to catch the next steamer that led them to us.

◆ ◆ ◆

After two more days on the river we arrived at a place where we unloaded the wagons and started once again across the land, but we knew we were getting close to our new home. Papa blew the trumpet with a renewed strength to set us on our way. The

42

trails were rough through thick forests and the steady rain for several days soaked us through and through. But our spirits and hopes were not dampened. Even though Willie rode in silence ahead of us all, there was an increased feeling that he too was reaching his new home.

When we came upon a stream that I heard someone call the Willapa, we heard shouts from ahead and saw a small group coming out to meet us. Papa blew his trumpet and we all were lifted by the notes of jubilation. But Papa quickly commanded silence and he raised his voice in prayer to thank the Lord for allowing us to complete this journey. Just as Papa was finishing his solemn words I caught a glimpse of a woman standing next to a small child. I realized that this was Emma. I was elated to see her but she did not look like the same person I said goodbye to in Missouri. She seemed smaller and looked very tired. But her eyes still sparkled when she saw me.

◆　◆　◆

Still today I remember the joy I felt at seeing Emma again and meeting her child. That was about the only joy I felt as the new beginning at Willapa was for me and many others from our wagon train as dark as the weather was in this new country. Even now—seven years later—I grow sad thinking about the brief time we spent along the Willapa River. Mama says remembering is good but I must rest before remembering these times.

◆　◆　◆

Although I paid no heed to the date we arrived at Willapa, most colonists now know it was November 1, 1855, as the very next day a new colonist joined our group. One of the women who traveled five months over the long trail had been with child and the baby arrived at Willapa soon after we did. There was much joy over this event and several saw it as a strong sign that the new beginnings at Willapa would be blessed ones. Mama, in particular, was pleased at this birth coming after such a long journey following the wagon with Willie's box.

But the joy did not last long, as it became apparent very early in our time at Willapa that Papa did not approve of the location selected by Christian Giesy and the other scouts. Although he did not express his feelings directly with his children, it was clear that Papa was not pleased and Mama told us that Papa was unhappy with Christian's choice and that a new place must be found. It was also difficult for Papa, she said, and for all of us as we must find a final resting place for Willie soon.

The dark clouds of late autumn, and the nonstop rain, made the moods of all at Willapa much lower than what we had eagerly anticipated back at Bethel and what had encouraged us on the difficult journey west. At times I was glad that Willie was not with us as he likely would have been the most disappointed of all as his hopes had been so high. And then, of course, I realized that Willie was still with us.

We remained in our wagons and in a few hastily constructed buildings that could hardly be called houses. As if there were not enough gloom, one day Papa announced it was time to say goodbye to Willie. Preparations were made to bury Willie on a small hill that overlooked the Willapa River among a small grove of trees. On the selected day, even darker and rainier than most, a solemn procession followed Willie one more time to the small hill and with prayers and song Willie's box was lowered into the ground. I stayed close to Mama as she quietly wept and said her goodbyes to her first child. I know she would have said this was a new beginning but she was silent and remained so for several days.

❖   ❖   ◆

That is all I care to remember of Willapa. I know Willie still
rests there but I like to think of him—and Mama—in happier
places. I do not wish to see Mama so sad again as she was then.
I hope I am well soon and can make Mama happy as I know
she worries about me.

❖   ❖   ◆

1857

Now I stand in God's creation
As a stranger, as a guest
And now my creator calls me.
I seek my peace in you.

The months after we laid Willie to rest are as blurry to me now as the shadowy figures that silently move in and out of the room to change the cloth on my forehead or to give me sips of water every now and then. I know who these women must be but in the darkened room I cannot make out their faces and their whispered voices are too soft for me to determine who is speaking. Such were the three or four months—I'm not even sure which—we spent at Willapa. It was almost as if I had a fever during that time but I think it was a fever shared with almost everyone who came with us on the wagon train.

I do remember spending some time with Emma but even that was not as happy a time as I wished. Emma was quite sad—and even a little angered—that Papa had rejected the site that her Christian had selected for the colony. In fact, Emma stayed away from visiting with Mama after she helped console Mama following Willie's burial. Everything seemed all wrong in this place and even hopes of a new beginning seemed to unravel as the winter slowly drew on and on with more rainy days than I think even Noah must have experienced.

Then Papa announced that we were moving south to Portland in Oregon Territory, back across the Columbia River. Crossing the Columbia again was enough to make my fears grow and the thought of moving to another unfamiliar place only heightened my anxieties. It seemed now that we were moving away from something instead of toward something and this did not seem right to me, as I am sure it did not seem right to many. But we did not question Papa, or at least most everyone did not, though a few families chose to stay at Willapa when the rest of us headed to Portland. This made things even more confusing and sad for me. Some were staying with Willie in his new home while his own family moved away. It all became a blur and remains so to this day.

◆ ◆ ◆

We travelled to Portland in early 1856 but that river crossing has faded from my memory. So too have many details of where we stayed in Portland other than that our larger group was scattered in various places. Papa took up some tailoring and also did some healing but he also travelled much to see if he could find a suitable place for us to gather again as a community and truly have a new beginning.

Then Papa returned one sunny spring day—or so it seemed like a sunny day—with the news that he had found two parcels of land along a small creek and close to a larger stream some twenty-five miles to the south of Portland. There already was a small mill at the site and there was timber available as well as good tillable land. As he was walking through this land, he told us, the skies opened up above him and the sun shone on the majestic, snow-capped mountain to the east—Mt. Hood—and Papa took this as a sign that this was a good place. He had signed the papers and came to tell us that we should begin preparations to move to this new site as soon as some buildings could be constructed. He informed those who could do the construction to head to the new place and begin work.

Mama was the happiest I had seen her in some time when Papa shared the news. She then asked him what he intended to call this new place. He looked around at Mama and all his children gathered to learn of his news and then he looked directly at me. He said in his loud voice but also almost as if in prayer, "I have decided to call it Aurora. It is the dawn of a new life for us. A new beginning."

◆ ◆ ◆

The words still send a shiver down my spine six years after he spoke them. I was overwhelmed at this declaration and I

49

continue to be. Did Papa always have this in mind? Was it why they chose to name me Aurora in the first place even though I don't think Papa was thinking of moving from Bethel when I was born? Did the sun shining on the mountain inspire him to choose this name? Did he receive divine guidance in making this choice? I feel guilty and too pompous at this last suggestion; why would the Almighty suggest my name over many others? Of course, Papa would never share his thoughts on why he selected Aurora as the name for our new Eden other than to say that it was the right choice. And I have never questioned him about it. I remain humble yet delighted that our new beginnings took place in Aurora. And still a shiver runs down my spine even as the rest of me burns with this fever.

◆　◆　◆

We travelled to the new site—it took me a while to call it Aurora—a few times in the next several months but we did not move there until early 1857, when our new house was mostly complete. Others had moved earlier and when we settled into our new home it felt more like a community than we had been for some time, even though the other buildings were scattered around the countryside. But it felt like the beginnings of a new life for us and, since it was now growing close to two years since we left Bethel, we all were ready for this new beginning. The excitement of this even made me forget for a time about Willie and his resting place but then I would think how excited he would be at this place called Aurora.

◆　◆　◆

There were many new beginnings in this beautiful place. One for me was that Mama decided I should learn to read and write, at least to be able to read scripture and to write my name and

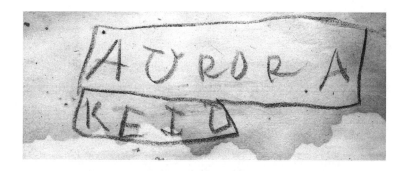

a few common things. Papa says he is not in favor of book learning—except for the Good Book—and he does not believe young girls needed to know these frivolous things, but he brought the schoolteacher, Mr. Ruge, with us on our journey so he must have thought learning was important. In her own way, Mama saw to it that Louisa and then Gloriunda learned a few things, although this was limited by the number of books in the colony, first in Bethel and even more so in Aurora. I think Mr. Ruge and others would have liked to bring more books with them but bringing such frivolous things on the wagon train would have made Papa very angry—even more than plates and dishes, which some tried to sneak on their wagons. At least plates and dishes have some use, according to Papa, while books did not. Of course, Papa had some of his own books but Mama said it was important for the colony leader to have such things.

My earliest instruction came from Louisa and Gloriunda but sometimes Mr. Ruge allowed me to look at his books. He also would let me practice writing in some of these since we had no writing tablets or other places to write except on the soft ground. The pages in the front and the back of books are where I learned to write my name.

I never showed my writing to Papa but I did take it to show Mama one day. She was very happy for me and hoped that this might be a new beginning for me. It made me feel warm to see Mama smile at my writing. I wish I could make Mama smile more often.

◆   ◆   ◆

I continued to take lessons from Mr. Ruge and up until I became ill was learning more about history and literature. Louisa and Gloriunda seemed less inclined for book learning but I found it a different way to discover new and exciting things. I am looking forward to getting well so I can continue in my schooling. The schoolteacher has some books on poetry that he says he will share with me so I can see how others have painted pictures with words. This sounds like something I would enjoy.

◆   ◆   ◆

My more useful instruction, at least as Papa saw it, was given by Mama and other women of the colony. This was in cooking, sewing and mending clothes, and, what was more exciting to me, quilting. I did enjoy this and I know Mama enjoyed teaching me what she knew. Louisa was already quilting some fine things and I did not think I could be as good as she was but Mama said it would come with time. I wanted to do needlepoint like the one Emma made for me but I still didn't have as much patience as I needed for this. Mama also said that this would come as I grew older. So much was about time and growing older and I often was too impatient for all of that, like I am now kicking the quilts off my bed.

◆   ◆   ◆

1859

Every little flower, every little tree
Are waiting only for our greetings
And the little lamb at pasture
Will always answer your call

Elias often teased me about our colony being named for me but Mama would tell me that I should tease him back and ask who would want to live in Elias. I never did though, probably because Elias was my favorite among my brothers—that is, of course, after Willie. I miss Willie so much sometimes and even though he has been gone now for many years I still expect to see him coming down the path. I even miss the wooden box that he rode in on our journey west, as it was something I could see every day to make me think of Willie. But that box is now in the ground on a hill above Willapa Bay and I don't even have that as a reminder of Willie. Mama says we will see Willie someday soon and I cannot wait to ask him about his own journey.

◆　◆　◆

With the arrival of my tenth birthday I expected big changes in my life and perhaps some new beginnings. In most ways, however, life continued about the same in our little community. Some buildings were constructed but Papa fretted that those who could really help Aurora grow remained at Bethel and his vision of a Second Eden was slower to be realized than he hoped. Of course, Papa never said this directly to us children but that's what Mama told us, particularly when Papa seemed more tired and spent more time alone in his room.

Mama also said Papa was concerned about the state of things back in Missouri because of how certain people were treated because of the color of their skin. This bothered Papa, and many others, Mama said, because it was un-Christian and especially counter to the Golden Rule. Mama said that even some ministers in Missouri and in other states did not treat black people in the same way as white people and, above all, this angered Papa.

Speaking of states, Oregon became one—the thirty-third, Mr. Ruge, the teacher, said. This happened a month before my birthday and I would not have paid it any mind except that the musicians of the colony were asked to play at the celebration that took place on February 14 in the town of Salem, several miles from Aurora. Mama said it was a great honor for the Aurora band to be invited to play at this event and even Papa was pleased about this one success of our colony. I think Papa was also pleased that the Aurora Colony was started even before Oregon was a state. When he and Mama came to the United States, they lived in states that had been founded at the time the country was formed. When Papa started the Bethel Colony, Missouri had been a state for almost twenty-five years. Now his new Eden had been established before Oregon became a state and this truly was a new beginning.

◆　◆　◆

1861

Oh if I could travel with you
Oh, you golden morning light
Never would I part from you
All time I would stay with you

Mr. Ruge told us of new beginnings for the United States as a man named Abraham Lincoln had been elected president. The teacher seemed pleased with this news and he said there was great hope for this man from Illinois who had grown up in humble surroundings in Kentucky. He showed us a picture from a newspaper of the man with a large hat. He certainly did not look like a president to me but then I'm not sure if I knew what a president should look like. I had seen pictures of George Washington and Thomas Jefferson, as they were in some of the books Mr. Ruge had, but Lincoln did not look like either Washington or Jefferson. I guess looks were not that important in becoming a president.

Not too long after this, the schoolteacher told us that the worst fears of many people, including several of the men at Aurora and others back in Bethel, had been realized. A war had started between many of the states back East and young men were dying as they fought over differences between the northern states and south. I noticed that Mr. Ruge and many of the other men of the colony seemed very somber since this news reached Aurora.

All of this seemed so far, far away, especially since it was in a place farther away than Bethel—and it had taken us five months to travel from there. How could these events on the other side of the country, as the teacher showed us on a map, have such an impact here in our colony? Mama tried to explain that the men still living in Missouri might have to fight and perhaps some of the young men in Aurora too. I told Mama that I did not think that war was fair and she responded that indeed not much is fair in wars. For the first time I felt relief that Willie was not still with us as he might have had to go off to fight. Of course, I was concerned for August, Fritz, and Eli too and did not wish to see them become soldiers, but I knew if Willie was still with us that he would find something to be excited about in going off to fight. The thought of that made me miss Willie again but I also had a sad sense of joy that we would not have to lose him again.

◆　◆　◆

A voice in the darkness rouses me from my recollections and I am grateful to have had my thoughts interrupted. A fresh damp cloth is placed on my forehead as the voice offers some soothing words of comfort. I recognize the voice but am too weary to realize who it is. My mind is clearer on the past than it is in the present, it seems. I close my eyes as I listen to the subdued words of encouragement.

◆　◆　◆

It's Emma! I remember thinking that my eyes surely were playing tricks on me on that warm summer day as I looked up from the spinning wheel where one of the colony women was showing me how to spin. Talking to Mama with three children beside her was a younger woman who looked like—had to be—Emma Giesy. Right here in Aurora! I practically knocked over the spinning wheel and the woman assisting me as I leapt up to get a closer look at the visitor. And it indeed was Emma with her two boys and two young daughters. Mama frowned as I interrupted her conversation with Emma but she smiled when Emma turned and gave me a big hug. Emma looked tired and somewhat in disarray but also seemed relieved to be here at the colony. And I was delighted to see her—and her children, as I had grown older and wiser in my understanding of the Golden Rule and in dealing with the changing ways of life.

Emma informed us that she was not just visiting but had decided to relocate to Aurora from Willapa since she lost her husband. This clearly was a new beginning for her and her children. For many of us in Aurora, especially me, it was a new beginning as well. We needed such a new beginning as we struggled with the news of the war and with the challenges of getting our colony to grow as it had at Bethel. Many good things were happening but there seemed to be a need for a new spark of life. Maybe Emma's arrival was that spark. At least it was for me, and I think it was for Mama as well.

◆ ◆ ◆

It's Emma, I thought to myself after the soft voice had stopped and the room became quiet again. That was Emma who was tending to me this last time. I wish I would have know it then, as I would have liked to visit with her. But my voice has mostly left me and only a dry rasp seems to come out when I try to speak. I tried calling to Louisa and Gloriunda earlier but nothing came from my mouth. Some nice soothing tea from the herbs in Mama's garden would feel so good, but I can only seem to swallow small amounts of water right now. My thirst is great at times but my stomach does not take kindly to food or water with this fever. I wish it would go away soon as I am ready to be better.

◆ ◆ ◆

1862

But alas, you hurry so fast
For you bring light to the world
Therefore I have to stay here
Goodbye, do not forget me.

The year started off with both fear and promise. There was still much talk among the men of the war in the East. These thoughts of war did not cause me great concern, particularly when I came to my thirteenth birthday in March. Papa does not allow us to celebrate much on these or similar personal occasions, but even he seemed to be in more happy spirits when my day arrived. Elias chided me about being an old maid but I knew his taunts were playful as he later gave me a small handful of early spring blossoms that he had gathered along the river.

◆　◆　◆

Although I am not certain of the date, or even the day of the week, I believe Amelia's and Emmanuel's birthdays are coming soon. Amelia will be twelve on the 17th and Emmanuel ten on the 18th. I think it is funny that of all the days in the year my younger sister and brother decided to join us on two adjoining days in December. But then Mama and Papa share the exact same birthday. Gloriunda and I were both born in March but several days separate our birthdays. Willie and Elias share the same birth month also—January—but they too had several days between their birthdays. Of course, I always remember when Willie left us in May just as much as I remember his birthday in January. Such are the things I think about as I lie under the quilts. I hope I am well enough to join the family for Amelia's and Emmanuel's birthdays. Mama always makes the day special in some way, even if it is an extra piece of bread at supper.

◆　◆　◆

Papa talks of more families from Bethel joining us in the coming year. This is exciting news for everyone but my memories of many of those people is very faint, like the dim December days.

But it will be good to have more of them joining us here in Oregon.

◆　◆　◆

The room has grown quieter and I no longer hear Louisa or Gloriunda near me with their coughs and soft moans, or the rustling quilts as they kick them off. Perhaps they are well and are up helping Mama with chores.

I do hear the gentle rain on the roof and it reminds me that it is the rainy time here in the valley of the Willamette. The cloudy, gray days are something I don't think I will ever get to like. Maybe it's because of my name but I like the sun and light.

◆　◆　◆

The room also has grown darker and at times I cannot tell if my eyes are open or closed. Mama says that sometimes one can see best when their eyes are shut. I am not sure what she means but I will look into the darkness and see what I can see.

◆　◆　◆

I see Willie walking ahead. Elias, Louisa, and Gloriunda are with him too. I think I will join them. It is a new beginning.

◆　◆　◆

AURORA KEIL

BORN

... 6, 1849

DIED

DEC. 14, 1862

New Beginnings

Temples stand, temples will fall,
Everything will turn to naught,
Nothing here can please me,
Without you, you golden light.

Aurora Keil joined her brother Willie on December 14, 1862. She was preceded in death by Elias, who passed away on November 22, 1862, and Louisa and Gloriunda, who both passed away on December 11, 1862. All four Keil children died of smallpox, a disease that claimed the lives of many settlers and Native Americans throughout early American history.

◆　◆　◆

Several months after Aurora's death, a wagon train of over two hundred and fifty followers of William Keil arrived at the Aurora Colony with many artisans and craftsmen to assist in the construction of buildings. The colony grew quickly after this, adding a church, hotel, and many houses. Both the church and the hotel were built with special balconies for the Aurora Band to entertain the community members and tourists who came to stay at the Aurora Hotel and to enjoy the excellent meals cooked by the women of the colony. The colonists also grew many orchards and other crops that brought attention to the excellent agricultural ways of the Aurora Colony. In 1870, the railroad arrived in Aurora and with it more tourists and others interested in the community named for the daughter of William Keil.

Aurora's younger sister, Amelia, died in 1872 of scarlet fever, having lived the longest—twenty-two years—of any of the Keil girls. William Keil died in late 1877 and his wife, Louisa, died in July 1879. By then the Aurora Colony was in the process of dissolving and by 1883 it no longer existed. Ten years later, however, the town of Aurora was established, still honoring the daughter of the dawn and with hopes of new beginning

Afterword

Jim Kopp was always a great storyteller. So when he told me he planned to write a novel for children about Aurora Keil and the eponymous late-nineteen-century colony south of Portland, Oregon, I knew it would be a gem. And it is. He generously shared drafts with me and kindly incorporated some of my suggestions. When he was given the chance to have a classroom teacher read his draft to the age group the story targeted, Jim jumped at the opportunity. The teacher had the children write postcards to him about their reactions. Those of us fortunate to read those penned missives marveled at their insights and Jim's willingness to again incorporate ideas he knew would make the story stronger and help inspire an interest in history for those young readers.

As he wrote, Jim and I often spoke of finding ways to promote our stories about Aurora and the colony and I looked forward to having *Aurora, Daughter of the Dawn*, on my book table when I spoke around the country about this unique community and the role that Aurora played in it. Jim, in turn, had already written on the academic level about the significance of novels in historical research, highlighting my own trilogy based on the Aurora Colony. The publication of his article in the *Oregon Historical Quarterly* brought new readers to my life. We spoke of events we might share in bringing Jim's *Aurora* to an audience of young readers.

Those of us who knew Jim and shared his passion about the Aurora Colony will forever lament that he did not live to see the light in kids' eyes as they read his charming story. But those of us wanting to carry his story forward will have the privilege of telling an important Oregon piece of history knowing that Aurora Keil has stepped from her generation into our own.

Jane Kirkpatrick

author of a trilogy of novels about the Aurora Colony:
A *Clearing in the Wild* (2006)
A *Tendering in the Storm* (2007)
A *Mending at the Edge* (2008)

and

Aurora: An American Experience in Quilt, Community, and Craft (2008)

History of Aurora Colony

One of the more successful American utopian communal societies in the nineteenth century was founded on the Pudding River in Marion County in 1856. Named for a daughter of the leader of the Christian communal group, the Aurora Colony (or Aurora Mills, as it was also known) grew to a population of more than 600 individuals who followed the basic Christian beliefs of Wilhelm Keil (1812-1877). The Aurora Colony became known for its orchards, food, music, textiles, furniture, and other crafts as well as its communal lifestyle and German traditions.

Keil was a Prussian-born tailor who also practiced apothecary and became a preacher and leader of souls. Arriving in the United States with his wife Louisa in the mid-1830s, at a peak of a religious revival, Keil sought his calling among several Protestant groups. Ultimately, he denounced all organized religion to establish a primitive Christian group devoted to the Golden Rule. After living in New York City and Pittsburgh for several years, in 1844 he sent a party west to find a suitable location to establish a colony where his followers could put into practice their common beliefs. They selected a site in Shelby County, Missouri, to establish the Bethel Colony, where Keil led nearly eight hundred individuals at its peak, with several satellite communities.

In 1853, Keil sought a new location for the colony and sent a scouting party to the Pacific Northwest. The scout group chose a location on Willapa Bay in Washington Territory, and in 1855 Keil led a party across the Oregon Trail to the new site. At the head of the wagon trail was a hearse carrying the body of Keil's oldest son, Willie, who had died shortly before the group left for the Northwest.

Keil was dissatisfied with the Willapa location and, despite burying his son there, chose to move south to Portland with many of his followers. In 1856, he purchased a donation land claim on the Pudding River, and the Aurora Colony became the new home for his followers. Bethel continued as part of the communal experiment under Keil's indirect leadership. In 1862, a smallpox epidemic struck the colony, and Keil lost four more of his children, including Aurora, after whom he named the colony.

At its peak, the population of the Aurora Colony grew to 600 from the 250 who left Bethel to follow Keil west. Aurora was slow to develop until 1863, when a large contingent arrived from Bethel. The group included carpenters and craftsmen who would lead the rapid build-up of the colony. Keil continued to serve as leader of the community, but in 1866 he drew up an agreement that would transfer control of the colony to a group of trustees. The trustees wrote "Articles of Agreement" that served as the constitution for the colony.

Keil was instrumental in bringing the Oregon & California Railway line to Aurora in 1870. The railroad connected Aurora with other cities and brought more business to the Colony Hotel, as well as spreading the word about the offerings at Aurora. The Aurora Colony Band became famous on the West Coast and traveled to many locations to play music, much of it written by Aurora musicians.

In the early 1870s, after the death of his only remaining daughter, Keil began to transfer ownership of several parcels of colony land to individual households, with the intent to transfer more later. Keil died suddenly on December 30, 1877, without having made any further transfers. The trustees assumed leadership of Aurora and Bethel and decided to dissolve the two colonies, a process that took several years and was overseen by Judge Matthew P. Deady. The final settlement of the dissolution was declared on January 22, 1883.

Ten years after the dissolution of the Aurora Colony, the City of Aurora was incorporated. Many colony descendants continued to live in the area, and several colony buildings survived, although the Colony Church, the Gross Haus (Keil's home), and the Colony Hotel were among those lost to fire and demolition. In 1963, a group of descendants and other interested individuals formed the Aurora Colony Historical Society to preserve the buildings and artifacts of the Colony. In 1966, the Old Aurora Colony Museum was dedicated, and in 1974 twenty sites in Aurora were placed on the National Register of Historical Places. It was the first historic district of its kind in the state.

by Jim Kopp from the Oregon Encyclopedia
By permission of Oregon Historical Society and Portland
  State University

For more information on the Aurora Colony see
www.auroracolony.org

About the Artist

Clark Moore Will, whose father and foster parents were members of the Aurora Colony, had a life-long interest in its history and documenting it for the future. He was a self-taught artist; his illustrations of the journey from Missouri and daily life in the community, as well as the architecture, have greatly enhanced our understanding of the Aurora Colony.

Will's papers are at the University of Oregon Libraries, Special Collections & University Archives.

Guide to the Clark Moore Will Papers, 1871-1981, http://nwdadb.wsulibs.wsu.edu/findaid/ark:/80444/xv05822